The WEREWOLF CLUB

#3

The
WEREWOLF CLUB

#3

The Werewolf Club
Meets Dorkula

DANIEL AND JILL PINKWATER

ALADDIN PAPERBACKS
New York London Toronto Sydney Singapore

First Aladdin Paperbacks edition June 2001

Aladdin Paperbacks
An imprint of Simon & Schuster
Children's Publishing Division
1230 Avenue of the Americas
New York, NY 10020

Book design by Corinne Allen
The text for this book was set in Weidemann Book.
The illustrations were rendered in Magic Marker,
pen, and imported European wolf spit.

Printed and bound in the United States of America

10 9 8 7 6 5 4 3 2

CIP Data for this book is available from the Library of Congress.

ISBN: 0-689-83847-6

CHAPTER ONE

The members of the Watson Elementary School Werewolf Club were sitting around the outdoor fireplace in Mr. Talbot's backyard, barbecuing veggie burgers. Mr. Talbot is our faculty sponsor. It may seem strange for a bunch of werewolves to be eating veggie burgers, but we had sort of lost our taste for the real thing. Not long before, we had eaten some really huge meatballs when we saved Earth from evil space aliens. These space aliens had taken the form of meatballs, and we had no choice but to eat them. When I say huge, I mean as big as a person.

Mr. Talbot's mother appeared with a large bowl. "Who would like some nice chicken necks?" she asked.

"Ack!" said Lucy Fang, the only female member of the Werewolf Club.

"Ick!" said Ralf Alfa, the handsome and athletic natural leader of the Werewolf Club.

"Ook!" said I, Norman Gnormal, the newest member of the Werewolf Club.

"Fried or stewed?" asked Billy Furball, the most unsanitary member of the Werewolf Club.

"By the way," Billy Furball said. "Did you all know we have a vampire in our school?"

CHAPTER TWO

"A vampire?" Mr. Talbot asked. "That's ridiculous, not to mention impossible. There can't be a vampire in our school."

"Why not?" Lucy Fang asked.

"Because there is no such thing as a vampire," Mr. Talbot said. "Imagine! Sleeping in a coffin! Going around biting people! Turning into a bat! It's nothing but cheap fiction!"

"But we're werewolves," I said. "We turn into wolves. How is that so different from turning into a bat?"

"You compare a noble wolf to a dinky little bat?" Mr. Talbot asked. "It's completely different. Being a werewolf is a normal, healthy thing. We spend lots of time outdoors, getting exercise. We are close to nature. We do good deeds. How about the time you children saved Earth from those meatball-like space aliens? Werewolves are nothing like vampires. Vampires are just some sick movie writer's dream. Besides, they are not very nice people."

"I thought you said they didn't exist," Ralf Alfa said.

"They don't."

"Then how could they be not very nice people?" Ralf Alfa asked.

"That's another thing I don't like about them," Mr. Talbot said. "If you don't exist, then you should have the good manners not to go around being a bat, and biting people."

CHAPTER THREE

"What makes you think there's a vampire?" I asked Billy Furball.

"I met him. He told me."

"Did you see him change into a bat?"

"No, but he bit me."

"He bit you!"

"Well, he bit my juice box."

Billy Furball held up a juice box. It had contained his favorite: banana/clam. The juice box was empty and had two neat triangular holes in it.

"He bit it, and sucked out all the juice in two seconds," Billy Furball said.

"That's a neat trick, I'll admit," Mr. Talbot said. "But it doesn't make him a vampire."

"What did he do then?" Lucy Fang asked. "Did he flip his cape out like wings, turn into a bat, and fly out the window?"

"No," Billy Furball said. "He headed for the baseball diamond in the park."

"Oh, really? What position does he play?"

"He said he wasn't a player. He said he was the umpire."

"Billy Furball, you do know the difference between an umpire and a vampire, don't you?"

"Sure. One will turn off a batter by shouting like heck, and the other will turn into a bat and bite your neck."

"Did you tell us this whole story just to lead up to that stupid joke?" I asked Billy Furball.

"Well, yes," Billy Furball said. "But there really is a vampire. His family comes from Transylvania."

"We don't believe you."

"It's true! They're Romanian noblemen."

"We don't care if they're Romanian pastrami."

"Well, you'll see for yourselves," Billy Furball said. "He's coming to the next official meeting of the Werewolf Club."

CHAPTER FOUR

So it was that Henry Count Dorkula, a nasty little geek, attended the very next meeting of the Watson Elementary School Werewolf Club in Mr. Talbot's classroom after school.

"Whasssssup, canines!" Henry said. "I brought you all some goodies!" Henry had a bakery box full of what looked like raspberry jelly doughnuts, to which all werewolves are partial. When we bit into them, we discovered someone had sucked out all the raspberry filling through two neat little triangular holes.

"Hey! Somebody fanged all the jelly out of my Bismarck!" Ralf Alfa said.

"What did I tell you?" Mr. Talbot asked. "No manners, and nonexistent with it."

"I couldn't help it," Henry Dorkula said. "I'm a sucker for sweets."

"Not to be rude," Lucy Fang said. "And thanks for the un-jelly doughnuts . . . but why are you here? This is the Werewolf Club, you know."

"It was Mr. Pantaloni's idea," the undead geek said. "You know, the principal? I believe he's the head man in this school, and your boss, Mr. Talbot. He said I should come to meetings because you are the only other students who turn into animals."

"Ha!" Lucy Fang said. "He should visit the lunchroom around noon sometime. So, you're saying you turn into something?"

"Oho, yes!" Henry said. "Sometimes, I just go batty."

"Vampire bat?"

"Bat. Big bat. What's the difference?"

"I've got my suspicions about you, Henry Count Dorkula," Lucy Fang said.

CHAPTER FIVE

"Why do we have to put up with him?" Lucy Fang asked Mr. Talbot. "He's not even a werewolf."

"This is a public school," Mr. Talbot said. "Anybody can join any school club. You don't have to be a werewolf to be a member of the Werewolf Club."

"Yeah? Well, how come we never had any members who weren't werewolves before this?" Lucy Fang asked.

"The other kids have delicate stomachs?" I asked.

"Besides," Mr. Talbot said, "you forgot Norman Gnormal. Norman here wasn't a werewolf when he first joined the club."

"That's different," Lucy Fang said. "Norman was

11

raised by parents who really wanted a dog. He developed the right instincts from puppyhood, and never even slept indoors until he was three."

"And I turned into a real werewolf later," I reminded the others. They would still tease me sometimes when I would howl at fire engines or when my mother would pack dog biscuits with my lunch.

"Maybe Henry will turn into a werewolf, too," Ralf Alfa said.

"Fat chance, turkey," Henry Count Dorkula said. "A vampire is better than a werewolf. Especially me. I come from Romanian noblemen. My great-great-great-great uncle was a count *and* a vampire, *and* he also invented the dill pickle. His name was Noshferatu."

"Gee!" Billy Furball said.

CHAPTER SIX

"I'll tell you more reasons I'm better than you," Henry Count Dorkula said. "I can turn into a bat anytime I feel like it, whereas you guys have to wait for a full moon. As a vampire, I am naturally handsome and smooth, and girls can't resist me."

Henry Count Dorkula fluttered his eyelashes at Lucy Fang.

"Let's see you turn into a bat right now," Lucy Fang said. "And then you can go hang upside down somewhere."

"I don't happen to feel like it," Henry said. "I could if I wanted to, but I don't."

"I think you're a fake," Lucy Fang said. "What do you think, Mr. Talbot?"

"Well, I don't believe in vampires, as you know," Mr. Talbot said. "But Henry is certainly welcome to attend meetings of the Watson Elementary School Werewolf Club."

"And there you have it," Henry said. "You have to let me be a member—and no wearing garlic around your necks or driving wooden stakes through my heart. You have to be nice to me."

"We would never do those things," Ralf Alfa said. "And we will be nice to you."

"Right. You should be nice to me. Remember, I brought jelly doughnuts," Henry said.

"But you sucked the jelly out of them!" Lucy Fang said.

"You can't prove that. There could have been a mishap at the jelly doughnut factory," Henry said.

"Can you teach me to flap my eyelashes like that?" Billy Furball asked.

"Why do you want to be a member of a werewolf club if you don't want to be a werewolf?" I asked.

"It was Principal Pantaloni's idea," the little

14

Dorkula replied. "He says I should develop better social skills.

"Well, I have to be going. See you later, simpletons!"

"Wait! I'll go with you, Master!" Billy Furball said.

CHAPTER SEVEN

"Master? Billy Furball called him Master?" Lucy Fang asked, after Henry and Billy had gone. "What's with that? Master?"

"I saw something like this in a vampire movie," I said. "The vampire got this guy to be under his power. After that, the guy was sort of a slave, and sort of went insane—and he'd eat flies."

"Billy Furball does that already," Ralf Alfa said. "Anyway, he snaps at them."

"What do you think, Mr. Talbot?" Lucy Fang asked. "Do you believe he's a real vampire now?"

"Since there are no such things as vampires, I do not," Mr. Talbot said. "I believe there are vampire

17

bats in South America, but that's a different thing completely."

Something dark with flapping wings flew through the room. It came low over our heads and made us duck. Then it was gone. We didn't get a clear look at it.

"What was that?" I asked.

"I have to grade papers now," Mr. Talbot said. "The meeting is adjourned."

CHAPTER EIGHT

"Something's wrong," Lucy Fang said as we stood on the street in front of Watson Elementary School. "Why did our lovable and unsanitary Billy Furball go off with that little Dorkula?"

"And why did he call him Master?" I asked. "It's spooky."

"Mr. Talbot is no help," Ralf Alfa said. "He refuses to believe in vampires. He has a closed mind."

"And what was that thing that flew in and out of the classroom?" Lucy Fang asked. "It had to be a bat."

"A big bat," I said.

"My brain hurts," Ralf Alfa said.

"My brain hurts," Lucy Fang said.

"My brain hurts," I said.

"Awoooooooooo!" We howled the age-old howl of the tormented wolf.

Then, suddenly, we were running—not running like human elementary school students. We were running like wolfish elementary school students. We loped, we sprinted, we leaped over garbage cans and tricycles, mailboxes and parked cars.

The ancient wolf-wisdom trickled through our young semi-human minds. We could smell things humans could not smell, hear things humans could not hear, know things humans could not know. As we ran, we felt the bond with wild hunters, crafty and cunning, who had ruled the wild lands for thousands of years.

When we finally stopped, we were in the park a mile away from school, panting, muscles sore . . . but we had communed with our wolf-selves.

"So, did anybody figure it out?" Lucy Fang asked.

"Not me," I said.

"Me neither," Ralf Alfa said. "I still don't have a clue."

CHAPTER NINE

"Guess who I saw today."

"Billy Furball?"

"Yes! He was walking along, and he had a paper bag, he was eating—"

"Oh, no! You're going to say flies, aren't you?"

"He was eating—"

"Oh! Ick! Don't tell me!"

"He was eating—"

"No! I'm going to be sick!"

"Grapes."

"Grapes?"

"Grapes."

"He was eating . . . ?"

"Grapes."

CHAPTER TEN

The Watson Elementary School playground, morning. Members of the Werewolf Club are standing around, waiting for the bell.

RALF ALFA: Look! Here comes Billy Furball now!

LUCY FANG: He's carrying something. What is it?

NORMAN GNORMAL: It looks like a pineapple.

BILLY FURBALL: Greetings, fellow werewolves. See the nice pineapple I am bringing for my master?

LUCY FANG: By your "master," you mean that obnoxious little twerp, Dorkula?

BILLY FURBALL: He is great! He can turn into a bat. It is an honor to serve him. I bring him whatever he wants, juice, fruit pies, oranges, raisins.

RALF ALFA: So, what are you saying? You're his slave?

BILLY FURBALL: Yes. Slave.

NORMAN GNORMAL: Um, Billy, did Dorkula ever, by any chance, bite you?

BILLY FURBALL: Hey! Nobody bites me! You trying to insult me?

LUCY FANG: Come to think of it, who'd be willing to bite you?

BILLY FURBALL: I must go. My master may want blueberry muffins.

(BILLY EXITS)

ALL: Nope, nothing unusual about him.

CHAPTER ELEVEN

"I was worried," Lucy Fang said. "You know, vampires like to drink people's blood. They bite them on the neck, and suck it out. Then those people become slaves, or vampires, or something—I never got it quite straight."

"Yick!" I said.

"Yick!" Ralf Alfa said.

From an open window above us, we heard Mr. Talbot's voice. "I told you—there are no such things as vampires, and also . . . yick!"

CHAPTER TWELVE

The next day, Mr. Talbot was feeling put out because the school cafeteria was sold out of baked apples with raisins and prunes, the favorite lunch of mature werewolves. This was unusual, because ordinarily Mr. Talbot was the only person to select the baked apple with raisins and prunes, and the lunchroom ladies had to throw the rest away.

NO FRUIT TODAY

CHAPTER THIRTEEN

That weekend, there was a strange mishap, which ruined the annual festival of San Irvingo. This is a festival held in the part of town where large numbers of people from Toledo, Ohio, have settled, and they brought with them their quaint custom of pelting each other with overripe tomatoes. There are also fireworks, pizza, and brass bands. It's a popular event. For pelting purposes, two large trucks full of bruised, too-ripe, and gooshy tomatoes are brought in and parked outside of St. Irving's Freestyle Church. This time, on the morning of the festival, there wasn't a single tomato to be found. Someone . . . or something . . . had made off with them.

With nothing to throw at one another, the Toledo-ians couldn't get into the spirit of the festival, and everybody went home early.

CHAPTER FOURTEEN

That same weekend, the vice president of the United States came to town, to award The American Green-Thumb award to a local gardener, Mrs. Mildred Papescu, for raising a Hubbard squash the size of a Volkswagen in her backyard.

The mayor and the city council showed up. There was no brass band available, because those were all booked for the disastrous San Irvingo festival, so the mayor's office supplied a bagpiper. The newspaper photographers and the TV cameras were there to get pictures of the vice president arriving in a helicopter.

Everybody was there, except the squash. It was gone without a trace.

CHAPTER FIFTEEN

Carla Lola Carolina, the manager at Honest Tom's Tibetan-American Lunchroom, had whipped cream to put on top of the Tapioca Surprise, but was all out of cherries to put on top.

Billy Furball's mother made him jelly-and-onion sandwiches, instead of jelly-onion-and-banana, because there were no bananas in the stores.

Banana splits had to be made with hot dog buns at ice-cream parlors around town.

Tangerines were selling for five dollars apiece, and two and three families were getting together to share the price of a grapefruit.

The Salvation Army was handing out vitamin C tablets in the streets.

CHAPTER SIXTEEN

"Something is not as it should be," Lucy Fang said.

"Yes. I have an uneasy feeling," Ralf Alfa said.

"I think there may be a pattern emerging," I said.

"A pattern?" Mr. Talbot said. "I'll show you a pattern! This city is in the grip of the worst food shortage since the war with Canada!"

"We had a war with Canada?"

"Maybe it was Mexico," Mr. Talbot said. "I can't remember. Anyway, there's a serious fruit shortage. I had to trade my bicycle for a fig and a prune yesterday."

CHAPTER SEVENTEEN

"So, you're saying that fruit in all its forms, and certain vegetables, are disappearing, is that it?" I asked.

"You're a little slow today, aren't you?" Lucy Fang asked me.

"Well, I just wanted to make sure," I said. "It's a very odd thing to happen."

"Odd things happen, Buster," Lucy Fang said. "It was just a few weeks ago that we were dealing with evil space aliens in the shape of meatballs. I call that pretty odd."

"Don't remind me," I said. "I can still taste them—not that they were bad with a little catsup and pickle relish."

"You think it's aliens again? Already? So soon after the last adventure?" Ralf Alfa asked.

"It could be aliens—but I think it will be something more clever and unexpected," Lucy Fang said.

"Such as what?"

"Such as . . . I'm not sure. But, I know who I want to talk with next . . . a certain so-called vampire, and his slave who's always getting him fruit."

"Dorkula!" Ralf Alfa said.

"And Billy Furball!" I said.

CHAPTER EIGHTEEN

"Hey, Dorkula!" Lucy Fang shouted. "Come over here, you little . . . fellow."

Henry Count Dorkula smiled. "You can't resist my charms anymore, right? You want to be my girlfriend?"

"Something like that," Lucy said. "You're a vampire, is that correct?"

"I am," Henry said.

"And you can turn into a bat?"

The members of the Werewolf Club were standing around, witnessing this conversation.

"I can turn into a bat. I can fly. I can suck your blood . . . muahahaha!" Henry said.

"You're getting ahead of me," Lucy said. "I was

thinking of letting you put the tooth on me."

"You were?"

"Yes. Take your best bite. Give me the old canines, right here on the neck." Lucy tilted her head to one side, exposing her neck. Dorkula looked nervous. "Or . . . ," Lucy continued. "Would you rather have . . . this?"

Lucy held up a juicy-looking pear.

"Is that . . . is that one of those River Yenta pears? The ones you can't buy in stores?"

"Yep," Lucy said. "They only come in gift baskets from Larry and Barry, the fancy fruit basket experts. You have to mail away for them, and they cost a fortune."

Henry was drooling. "Those are the best pears there are," he said.

CHAPTER NINETEEN

"What's it going to be?" Lucy Fang asked Henry Dorkula. "You want a nice vampire snack, namely my blood? Or would you rather have this nice, big, juicy, sweet, expensive, fancy-dancy River Yenta pear, from the Yenta River Valley in Idaho?"

Henry was sweating. "Give me the pear! Give me the pear!"

Lucy tossed him the pear, and he sank his pointy little teeth into it, sucking noisily. "Ohhh! Mama mia! This is a good pear!" he said.

"You like the pear, don't you?" Lucy asked.

"Mmmm, yum [slurp]," Henry said.

"You like all kinds of fruit and juicy vegetables, don't you?"

"Mmmm, yum [gobble, slurp]," Henry said.

"And you never drank blood in your life."

Henry looked up, his chin covered with pear juice. "Well, technically speaking, um, no."

"And what kind of a bat is it you turn into?" Lucy asked.

"Fruit bat," Henry said very softly.

"I can't hear you. What kind of bat?"

"Fruit bat."

"So you really aren't a vampire at all, are you?"

"No."

"And what are you really?"

"Fruitpire."

"Not quite the same thing, is it?"

"No."

"Gentlemen of the jury, I rest my case," Lucy said. "He is a fruit bat. And unless I am very much mistaken, he can tell us something about the disappearance of all the fruit lately."

"Save the core for me, Master," Billy Furball said.

CHAPTER TWENTY

"You mean to tell us that Henry stole practically all the fruit in town?" Ralf Alfa asked.

"Well, he's a fruitpire. You heard him admit it," Lucy said.

"What did he do, eat it?" Ralf asked.

"For all I know," Lucy said. "You saw what he did to the pear."

Henry spat out a couple of seeds. "I didn't take all that fruit," he said.

"I'll bet, if you didn't take it, you know something about it," Lucy said. "Am I right?"

"Maybe," Henry said. "But why should I tell you?"

"Because you're a member of the Werewolf Club," Lucy said. "Unless it *was* you who took the fruit, in which case you're a criminal . . . a very weird criminal, but a criminal all the same . . . and then you *can't* be a member of the Werewolf Club."

"Don't tell them anything, Master!" Billy Furball yelled.

"It wasn't me," Henry said. "But you'd let me be in the club, even though I'm not a vampire?"

"Turning into a fruit bat is good," Lucy said.

"They're bigger than vampire bats," I said.

"And the idea of anyone drinking blood creeps me out," Ralf Alfa said. "I prefer you as a fruit bat."

CHAPTER TWENTY-ONE

"You're being very nice to me," Henry said.

"Why shouldn't we be nice to you?" Lucy asked.

"Well, I've been sort of obnoxious," Henry said.

"Hey! We're werewolves!" Ralf Alfa said. "We're all obnoxious. Norman Gnormal has doggy breath, Lucy Fang scratches her ear with her foot, I whimper in my sleep, and we all have fleas."

"And we're not housebroken," Billy Furball said.

"Billy," Lucy Fang said. "The rest of us are housebroken. Only you are not."

"Oh. I forgot," Billy Furball said. "But you get the point, Master. We other kids who turn into animals are not going to judge you."

"Okay, I'm going to tell you," Henry Count Dorkula said.

"Tell us who stole the fruit?"

"Yes."

"Tell."

"It was Noshferatu."

"Noshferatu, your great-great-great-great uncle?" I asked.

"Noshferatu who was a count and a vampire, and invented the dill pickle?" Billy Furball asked.

"Only he isn't a vampire," Henry said. "He's a fruitpire, same as me."

"Is?" Lucy Fang asked. "He lives?"

"He lives," Henry said.

"He must be pretty old," Ralf Alfa said.

"He's undead," Henry said.

"I guess those undead last a long time," Ralf said.

"Oh, he's the real thing," Henry said. "Wears a cape and everything."

CHAPTER TWENTY-TWO

"So why did he do it? Why did he take all the fruit?"

"He wanted it," Henry said. "Old people need fruit."

"And being undead . . . "

"He's really old."

"He has to stop. He has to stop taking all the fruit," Ralf Alfa said.

"It won't be easy to stop him," Henry said. "He's old and clever—and powerful."

"What if we just asked him to stop?" Billy Furball asked.

"He's crafty and subtle and dishonest," Henry said. "Oh! I forgot to mention sneaky. He's sneaky, too. If we ask him to stop, he'll agree, but he'll do it just the same."

"So what do we do? You'll help us, won't you, Henry?" I asked.

"It's not my help you need," Henry said. "You have to get one of these vampire-hunters."

"But he's not a vampire."

"That's true. You have to get a fruitpire-hunter."

"Do those exist?" I asked.

"I'm not sure," Henry said. "Maybe we should ask someone."

"Let's ask Mr. Talbot!" I said. "He's supposed to be our adviser. Let's get him to advise!"

CHAPTER TWENTY-THREE

"A fruitpire, you say?" Mr. Talbot said. "I hadn't considered that. Of course it all makes sense. A fruit-pire would naturally be the one to steal all the fruit. And you say he's your great-great-great-great uncle, Henry?"

"So, you believe in fruitpires?" I asked Mr. Talbot.

"Believe? Of course, I believe. They exist. It's like asking a person if he believes in grapefruit," Mr. Talbot said.

"Do you believe in grapefruit?" Billy Furball asked Mr. Talbot.

"I do," Mr. Talbot said. "And fruitpires are real. It's those other ones . . . vampires, which do not exist."

"Our education is in the hands of some very strange people," Lucy Fang said.

"The question is, what can we do about it?" Ralf Alfa said. "We ought to stop the fruitpire, and Henry says that won't be easy. We need help."

"And help we shall have!" Mr. Talbot said. "We will go to see Van Helsing!"

"Van Helsing, the student of the supernatural and professor of the improbable?"

"No! Van Helsing, the fruiterer!"

"What the heck is a fruiterer?"

"No time to talk! Let's go!"

CHAPTER TWENTY-FOUR

A fruiterer is a guy who sells fruit. We piled onto the uptown bus, and piled out when we got to Van Helsing's Produce Market, in the middle of the fruit-and-vegetable district. Of course, Van Helsing's was a sorry-looking place, because of the fruit shortage, and many of the other fruit stands and stores were deserted. Van Helsing's shelves were mostly empty, with just a few tired-looking tangerines, and some brown bananas nestled in the corners here and there.

In the office, at the back of the market, we found Dr. Hugo Van Helsing. He was examining an avocado pit with a magnifying glass, stroking his white mustache and saying, "Hmmm," a lot.

"Dr. Van Helsing," Mr. Talbot began.

"Ah, a bunch of werewolves . . . and what is this? A fruitpire!" Van Helsing said. "What an unusual group! Be warned, if you plan any foul play, I am armed! I have a banana in my pocket!"

"We come in peace," Mr. Talbot said. "These werewolves and this fruitpire are pupils in good standing at the Watson Elementary School, and I am a teacher, and the faculty sponsor of the Werewolf Club."

"My dear Watson Elementary!" Van Helsing shouted. "That is my old school! How may I help you? And would you like some moldy grapes? I'm afraid they're the best I can offer."

"You know of course, it is a fruitpire who is responsible for the recent outrages," Mr. Talbot said.

"Yes, I suspected as much. We are taught of these things in fruiterer's college," Van Helsing said. "But surely you are not going to tell me that it is this little lad who has done so much harm?" Van Helsing lifted Henry by the collar and looked at him through the magnifying glass.

"No, no, of course not," Mr. Talbot said. "Henry is one of our finest students, and a member of our club."

"Thanks, Mr. Talbot," Henry said.

"I would like some moldy grapes," Billy Furball said.

CHAPTER TWENTY-FIVE

"It is my great-great-great-great uncle, Noshferatu, sir," Henry Count Dorkula said. "He is the one who has taken most of the fruit—and many juicy vegetables. And I am prepared to rat on him, for the good of society."

"You are a fine boy, and a credit to all fruitpires," Dr. Hugo Van Helsing said. "You live by the code of the South American fruit bat, which teaches us: 'Never fang more than you can eat—and eat what you fang.'"

"You are wise," Dorkula said.

"You know where your great-great-great-great uncle sleeps?" Van Helsing asked Henry.

"Yes, I do," Henry said.

"We must destroy him," Van Helsing said.

"Destroy him? He's my uncle! I didn't know you wanted to destroy him!"

"It's a figure of speech," Van Helsing said. "I didn't mean that we will really destroy him—in any meaningful way. We will just drive a stake through his heart."

"Uh-uh! Nix! Nothing doing!" Henry said. "I am not helping anybody drive a stake through anybody's heart, especially my uncle."

"Did I say, 'drive a stake'?" Van Helsing giggled. "I meant to say, 'put a steak.' That's how you deal with fruitpires—you have to put a steak over their heart. Then they are powerless and will keep any promise they make in order to get you to remove the steak."

"What kind of steak?" Billy Furball asked. "Sirloin? Porterhouse? Filet mignon?"

"I suggest a Romanian steak," Van Helsing said. "It may be necessary to outflanken your uncle."

The Werewolf Club pelted the old fruiterer with moldy grapes.

"Enough light-hearted banter and horseplay!" Mr. Talbot said. "Henry, you must lead us to your great-great-great-great uncle's hiding place."

CHAPTER TWENTY-SIX

"He is not the same Noshferatu who invented the dill pickle so many decades ago?" Hugo Van Helsing asked Henry.

"The same," Henry said.

"Oh, how sad! A great mind, turned to evil! Where does he sleep?"

"He sleeps in the daytime, in a crypt, which is to say a tomb, which is to say a stone room under the Fruit and Vegetable Workers' Cemetery," Henry said.

"My father sleeps in the daytime," Billy Furball said.

"Is he a vampire? Is he a fruitpire?" we asked.

"No. He is a night watchman," Billy Furball said.

We whacked Billy Furball with overripe bananas.

"The Fruit and Vegetable Workers' Cemetery is nearby," Hugo Van Helsing said. "Let us go there now and give Noshferatu the steakaroonie before he awakens!"

"Let me get this straight," Mr. Talbot said. "We put a steak, as in a hunk of meat, on his chest . . . over his heart . . . and that will do what?"

"It will make him weak," Van Helsing said. "Fruitpires are complete vegetarians, and raw meat makes them feel all icky. In his weakened state we can make him promise to quit stealing fruit, and pay retail, and society will return to normal."

"So this is nothing like driving a wooden stake through a vampire's heart? Not that they exist," Mr. Talbot asked.

"Well, sneaking into the crypt will be fun," Van Helsing said. "Look! We've arrived! Be very quiet, everybody!"

CHAPTER TWENTY-SEVEN

Henry Count Dorkula led us through the cemetery, which was old and spooky. It was almost night, and there were long scary shadows. He led us to a little stone house, with an iron door. The name "Dorkula" was carved over the door. Van Helsing and Mr. Talbot pushed the heavy door open, and we went inside. There were stone steps that led down into the darkness. Van Helsing took a flashlight out of his pocket, and a Romanian steak in a plastic baggie. He handed the steak to Henry, saying, "The honor is yours. Redeem the name of Dorkula."

We began to descend the stairs. It was cold. I was scared. At the bottom of the stairs, in a little stone room, we saw Noshferatu asleep in a large clear plastic crisper. There was a nauseating smell of salad dressing.

"Steak him, my boy," Van Helsing said.

Henry crept forward, steak in hand. He hovered over the sleeping fruitpire and slowly raised the steak above his head.

"That you, nephew?" Oh, no! The monster was awake! His eyes, like olives with pimentos, fluttered open, his lips drew back, revealing spinach caught in his teeth.

Henry lunged for his great-great-great-great uncle. "You have to quit boosting fruit, Unc!" he cried.

But he was not quick enough. In an amazing burst of speed, the undead fiend leaped from his crisper and rushed past Henry, and all of us, and sprinted up the stairs. I smelled avocados, and felt his cloak brush me as he sped past.

"After him! After the fiend!" Van Helsing shouted.

We stumbled up the stairs in the darkness, and emerged from the little tomb in time to see Noshferatu's cape flutter as he dashed through the cemetery gate.

CHAPTER TWENTY-EIGHT

"After him! After him!" Van Helsing shouted.

"After him! After him!" Mr. Talbot shouted.

"After him! After him!" Henry Count Dorkula shouted.

"After him! After him!" Ralf Alfa shouted.

"After him! After wooo!" Lucy Fang shouted.

"Afterwooo! Afterwooo!" I shouted.

"Awooooooo! Awooooooo!" Billy Furball shouted.

The full moon was rising, and we were turning into wolves.

Except Van Helsing, who had to stretch his long legs and work hard to keep up . . . and Henry, who turned into a large brown bat and flew over our heads.

"After him! After him!"

"Awoooo! Awoooo!"

"Squeak! Squeak!"

CHAPTER TWENTY-NINE

The werewolf pack, in full cry, followed the Amazonian fruit bat into which our Henry had turned. We could hear Henry's squeaks as he followed his great-great-great-great uncle, Noshferatu. We could hear Van Helsing huffing and puffing behind us, as he did a remarkably good job of keeping up . . . for a human.

Why had Noshferatu not transformed? Why wasn't he a bat? Why was he running instead of flying? He could run pretty well, I must say. He was keeping ahead of a bunch of more or less four-legged creatures, who wanted to catch him.

We ran along avenues and up and down streets. We ran through parks and backyards. We ran through the briars and we ran through the brambles. We ran through the bushes where a rabbit couldn't go.

We ran down to the waterfront, following Henry, the bat. Then we saw Noshferatu. He was getting onto a tugboat that was hitched up to a barge. The barge was full of Oregon grapefruit. He was going to try to steal one more bunch of fruit, while getting away!

Noshferatu shook his fist at us. He shouted up to Henry in bat-form, "Join me, nephew! I have enough Oregon grapefruit to satisfy your wildest dream!"

Noshferatu was at the wheel of the tugboat. Tugboats are fast, and even pulling the barge full of grapefruit, he was moving away from the dock at a good rate of speed.

CHAPTER THIRTY

Panting and drooling, the werewolves, and Van Helsing, came to a stop at the water's edge. There was no question of swimming after the tugboat—it was already too far out, and moving too fast.

We heard Noshferatu's crazed laughter. "I have escaped you, puppy dogs! Nothing can stop the fruit-pire!"

Then we heard a horrifying scream. Some kind of struggle was taking place on the boat. We heard someone shrieking—we hoped that was Noshferatu—and high-pitched squeaks—that would be Henry as a bat.

We stood at the water's edge, not able to do anything. Uneasy and frustrated, we slowly turned back into humans. The tug and the barge were not moving, just bobbing in the water.

Then, we heard the mighty engine come to life. The tug started pulling the barge. It was moving away from us! Oh, no! Noshferatu must have defeated Henry! But . . . wait! It was making a big circle! It was turning! It was headed back to the dock!

At the wheel we saw Henry! He had resumed his usual shrimpy human form. Sitting on the deck, with an odd expression, was Noshferatu.

Henry pulled alongside the dock and threw us a line. We helped tie up the tugboat. Then Henry marched his great-great-great-great uncle ashore.

"I steaked him," Henry said. "I steaked him good."

"That you did, nephew," Noshferatu said.

"I made him promise," Henry said. "Wholesale fruit theft is out, right, Unc?"

"And a fruitpire always keeps his word," Noshferatu said. "Especially when his own great-great-great-great nephew holds an icky steak over his heart, and forces him to promise."

"No hard vealings, right, Unc?" Henry asked.

"None at all, my boy. I hope someone steaks you someday is all," the old fruitpire said.

"This has been a fine night's work," Van Helsing said. "I invite you all, including Mr. Noshferatu, to be my guests at Honest Tom's Tibetan-American Lunchroom."

"You know that place?" Mr. Talbot asked.

"It's the best in town," Van Helsing said.

"I'm going to have pancakes with fruit on them," Billy Furball said as we were walking in the direction of Honest Tom's Tibetan-American Lunchroom.

"Yummm," Noshferatu said.

"So, how come Henry Count Dorkula was able to make Billy Furball his abject slave?" Mr. Talbot asked.

"He fed me," Billy Furball said. "Anybody could have done it."

END

Have you read the first two books in

The Werewolf Club

Series?

The WEREWOLF CLUB

#1

The Magic Pretzel

CHAPTER MINUS THREE

FREQUENTLY ASKED WEREWOLF QUESTIONS

Q: What is a werewolf?

A: A werewolf is a person who turns into a wolf from time to time.

Q: Is that true?

A: Would I lie to you?

Q: What makes a person turn into a werewolf?

A: Everyone knows people turn into werewolves if they are bitten by a werewolf, but you can turn into a werewolf by:

1. thinking about werewolves

2. using a drinking fountain after a werewolf

3. reading a book like this one

4. for no reason at all

Q: What should you do if a werewolf bites you?

A: Go home and wait.

Q: Are werewolves nice?

A: Oh, they are very nice. Of course, their ways are different from ours. Just remember, a bite can be a werewolf's way of saying, "Let's be friends."

Q: Is there any way to stop turning into a werewolf?

A: Yes. One.

Q: What is it?

A: It is the magic pretzel.

Q: The magic pretzel? Does such a thing really exist?

A: No one knows.

The
WEREWOLF CLUB
#2
The Lunchroom
of Doom

CHAPTER ONE

WEREWOLF? WHERE?

After the werewolf ate the whole fourth-grade class, and their teacher, the people of the village of Fangdorf began to feel uneasy. There had been werewolves in the Black Forest for years and years, but never one as scary as this.

Old Hans, the woodsman, was good at hunting and tracking. He followed the footprints left by the werewolf.

"These paw prints will lead us to the werewolf's lair," Old Hans said. "Then we will catch it and make a werewolf stew with onions and potatoes. Yum."

The paw prints led not deep into the forest but back to the village. They led right up the main street, to the house of Old Hans's grandmother.

Through the window, Old Hans and the villagers saw the werewolf. At first they thought it had eaten the old lady, but then they saw it change into Old Hans's grandmother.

"My old granny is the werewolf?" Old Hans said. "Now I understand why she was always scratching."

The villagers ate the old lady with potatoes and onions, but it was a sad occasion, because they had always liked her.

And the werewolf of Fangdorf was never seen again.